Table of Contents

What Makes a Family?   3

Photo Glossary   15

Index   16

About the Author   16

Rourke
Educational Media
rourkeeducationalmedia.com

Can you find these words?

adoption

birth

group

wedding

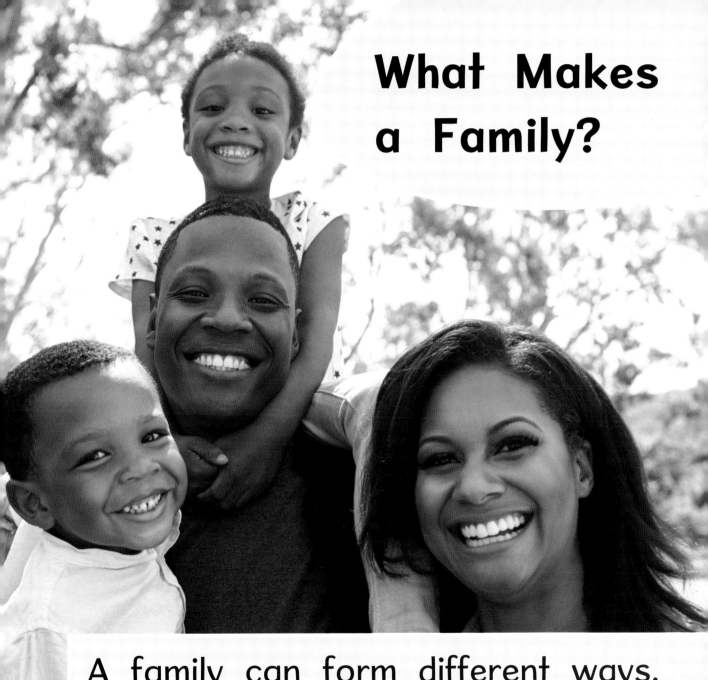

What Makes a Family?

A family can form different ways.

birth

Birth makes a family.

Adoption makes a family.

wedding

A **wedding** makes a family.

Love makes a family.

A family is a special **group** of people.

Did you find these words?

Adoption makes a family.

Birth makes a family.

A family is a special **group** of people.

A **wedding** makes a family.

Photo Glossary

adoption (uh-DAHP-shun): To bring a person into a family.

birth (burth): When a baby is born.

group (groop): People or things that go together or have something in common.

wedding: (WED-ing): When two people get married, they have a wedding ceremony.

Index

adoption 6

birth 4, 5

form 3

love 11

special 12

wedding 9

About the Author

Tammy Brown writes books and teaches teachers how to teach their students to read. She enjoys traveling with her husband and playing hide-and-seek with her grandchildren.

www.rourkeeducationalmedia.com

PHOTO CREDITS: Cover: ©monkeybusinessimages; p. 2,6,14,15: ©MissHibiscus; p. 2,4,14,15: ©monkeybusinessimages; p. 2,12,14,15: ©pixelheadphoto; p. 2,8,14,15: ©sirtravelalot; p. 3: ©monkeybusinessimages; p. 10: ©fstop123.

Edited by: Keli Sipperley
Cover design by: Kathy Walsh
Interior design by: Rhea Magaro-Wallace

Library of Congress PCN Data
What Makes a Family? / Tammy Brown
(Time to Discover)
ISBN (hard cover)(alk. paper) 978-1-64156-208-9
ISBN (soft cover) 978-1-64156-264-5
ISBN (e-Book) 978-1-64156-312-3
Library of Congress Control Number: 2017957906

Printed in the United States of America, North Mankato, Minnesota